D0409612

28 JAN 2013

The Scary Chef's
Scarecrow

by Martin Remphry

FRANKLIN WATTS
LONDON•SYDNEY

First published in 2011 by
Franklin Watts
338 Euston Road
London
NW1 3BH

Franklin Watts Australia
Level 17/207 Kent Street
Sydney
NSW 2000

A CIP catalogue record for this book is available
from the British Library.

ISBN 978 0 7496 9470 8 (hbk)
ISBN 978 0 7496 9476 0 (pbk)

Series Editor: Jackie Hamley
Series Advisor: Catherine Glavina
Series Designer: Peter Scoulding

Printed in China

Franklin Watts is a divison of
Hachette Children's Books,
an Hachette UK company.
www.hachette.co.uk

For my darling Sarb
M.R.

The chef loved his
vegetable garden.

But the birds loved his vegetables, too!

"Scare those birds away!"
demanded the chef.

The kitchen porters
jumped.

They made a scarecrow
and put it in the garden.

But the birds were
not scared of it at all.

"Scare those birds away!" shouted the chef.

The kitchen hand jumped.

She ran into the garden
and waved her spoon
at the birds.

11

But the birds flew off
with the spoon!

"Scare those birds away!"
yelled the chef.

The waiters jumped.

They took some rolls and
threw them at the birds.

But the birds dropped
something on the waiters!

17

The chef stamped his feet. "Can nobody scare those birds away?" he bellowed.

19

The dish washer
had an idea.

She found the chef's old apron and hat.

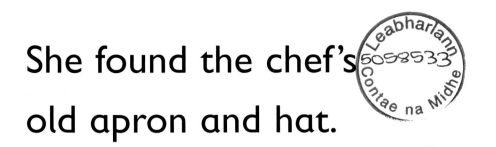

The porters dressed
the scarecrow in the
chef's clothes.

23

All the birds flew away!

"Well done!" cried
the chef.

27

"But I don't understand,"
said the chef.

"That scarecrow isn't scary at all!"

29

Puzzle 1

Put these pictures in the correct order.
Now tell the story in your own words.
How short can you make the story?

Puzzle 2

quiet   angry

furious

clever   wise

silly

Choose the words which best describe each character. Can you think of any more? Pretend to be one of the characters!

Answers

Puzzle 1

The correct order is:

1f, 2c, 3b, 4a, 5e, 6d

Puzzle 2

Chef The correct words are angry, furious.
The incorrect word is quiet.

Dish washer The correct words are clever, wise
The incorrect word is silly.

For details of all our titles go to: www.franklinwatts.co.uk

*hardback